MAGIC
in the AIR

Written by Renae Lopez-Buckley
Illustrated by Victoria Baskin Coffey
Design by Suzan Freeman

Foreword

Pregnancies should be the best of times, but can be the worst of times.
Sadly, for many families, their pregnancies don't progress as expected and hopes and plans are shattered.

These events remain with us and are part of who we are.
Our dreams will always be with us and no matter what direction our lives take, our children remain in our minds.
These thoughts and feelings are often difficult to express, even to those closest to us.

I hope this book helps your family recognise the place your child has in your hearts.

Professor Jon Hyett Head of High Risk Obstetrics, Royal Prince Alfred Women's and Babies Hospital

Message from a mother

Losing someone special is one of life's most difficult experiences.

You never get over losing someone special in your life, you only learn to live with it.
Finding the words to explain how you feel and what it means can be hard.

I hope this book will help to give you the words to explain the loss to your children.

I lost my son Alistair and wrote this book to help explain to my two daughters
where their brother is and what he means to our family. This book is dedicated to him
and all the precious souls who are shining so brightly in our hearts.

With special thanks to Amy Murphy for helping me develop the
ideas and giving me the confidence to create this book.

Renae Lopez-Buckley

Personalise and dedicate your book

This book has been designed to be personalised.

On the last page of the story write your
loved ones name in the star.

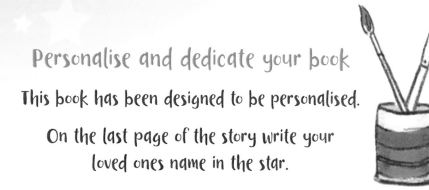

I am all dressed up to start my day,
but there is something
very important missing...

I peer into my toy box and feel around
searching for my special wand.

Abracadabra!

Dad's bike is big,
black and shiny.

He calls it Harley.
My friend Leo and I
laugh and giggle.

Dad starts Harley and it rumbles and roars like a lion.

There is something magic in the air, it follows me here...

and it follows me there.

I wrap a gift
for my friend's birthday party.

I found the most spectacular glittery paper.

I love to wrap gifts for my friends

it's so much fun!

Indie and I slide down the slippery slide.

weeeeeeee

Indie's Dad gives us a kite.
He tells us if we run very fast
the wind will pick up our kite taking it up, up, up, high into the sky.

There is something magic in the air,
it follows me here...

and it follows me there.

I love talking to my Poppy, he always has a funny story to tell me when I visit.

He is a very clever Poppy,
he can always give me a chocolate
ever so quietly so my
Mum doesn't see. Shhhhhhh

I visit the art gallery with Grandma.
She wants to show me her favourite painting.
We stand quietly and look,

it is beautiful and magical.

I notice a tear in her eye.

I reach up
and hold her hand.

There is something magic in the air,
it follows me here.

and it follows me there.

Today at school we had to colour in all these shapes, we had to choose our own special colour... Mine is green.

When we finished the teacher put our shapes together and it formed the most beautiful, wonderful star!

I walk along the beach with my Mum.
We love to collect shells,
make sandcastles

and chase the water.

Before we go Mum
makes a pattern in the
sand with our shells.

There is something magic in the air,

it follows me here and it follows me there.

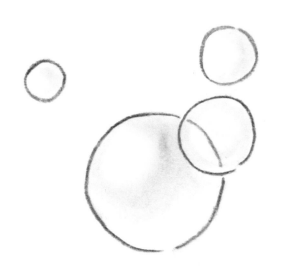

I jump into bed,
Mum pulls my covers up
and tucks me in.

I look out the window and see the biggest
and brightest star looking at me.

"Mum and Dad" I ask, "why have I seen all these stars"?
"Tell me, where have you seen them" asks Dad.

My wand
has a star on it

My paper for the
present had stars on it

Poppy and I may have
eaten one or two

Dad, there is one
on your bike

Indie's kite has
stars on it

They are in Grandma's
favourite painting

We made the most
beautiful star at school

Mum, you left one
at the beach

"Why are there stars all around me

And that big one looking at me" I ask.

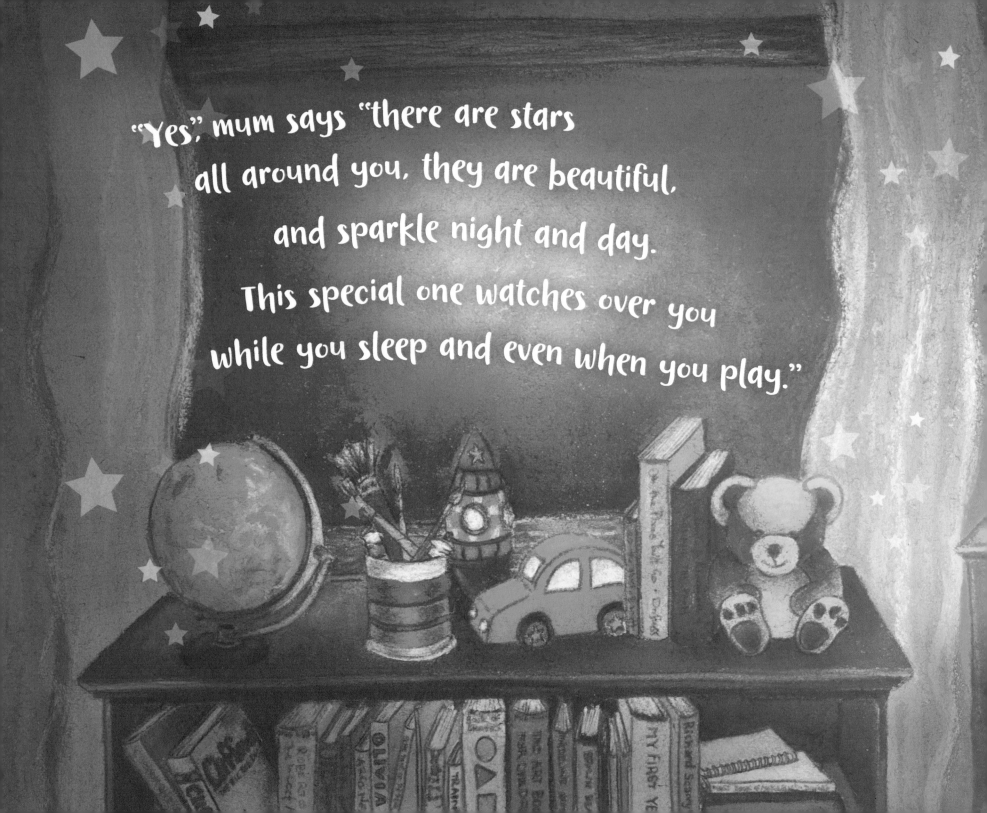

"Yes," mum says "there are stars
all around you, they are beautiful,
and sparkle night and day.

This special one watches over you
while you sleep and even when you play."

There is something magic in the air,

it follows me here and follows me there.

love will be with
me everywhere.

CPSIA information can be obtained
at www.ICGtesting.com
Printed in the USA
BVRC101737020521
606292BV00002B/2